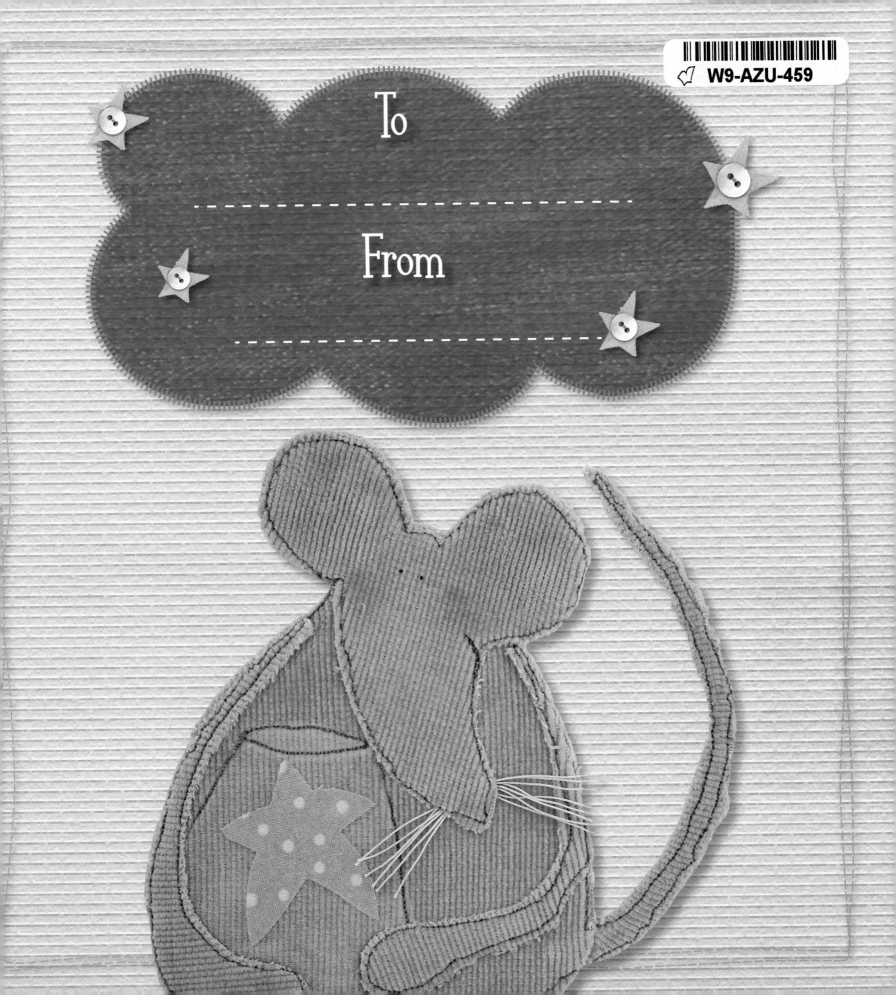

To

From

With thanks to Jane Horne

Copyright © 2007

make believe ideas

The Wilderness, Berkhamsted,
Hertfordshire, HP4 2AZ.

TWINKLE TWINKLE
LITTLE STAR

KATE TOMS

make
believe
ideas

Twinkle, twinkle,

little **star**,

How I wonder

what **you** are,

I'd love to catch you in my net...

Twinkle, twinkle,
little **star**,
I do so **wonder** what **you** are.

When snuggled up in bed at night,
Cozy, warm, and tucked up tight,

z z z Z

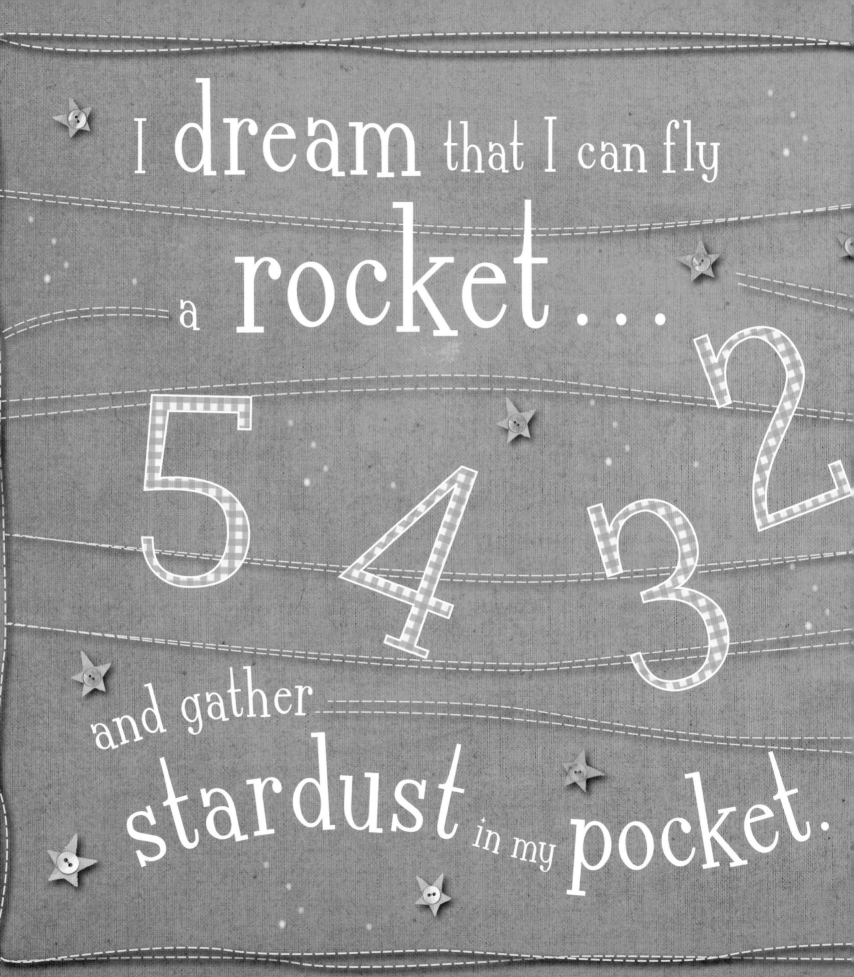

Twinkle, twinkle little **star**, How I wonder what **you** are.

Does a **man** live on the **moon**?

And if the **moon**

Yummy!

is made of **cheese**,

Twinkle, twinkle, little star,

What do you see from afar?

Hola!

Hello

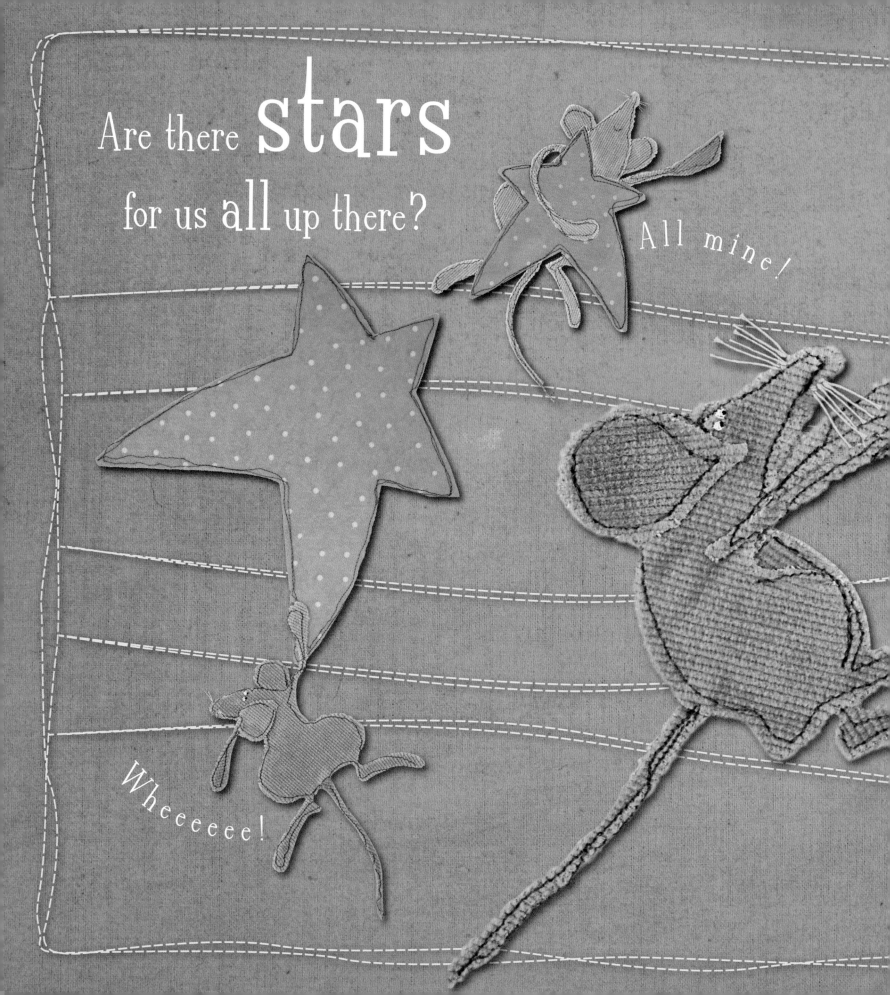

Are there **stars** for us **all** up there?

All mine!

Wheeeeee!

Jump!

Or do some folks have to share?

Twinkle, twinkle,

little star,

How I wonder

what you are!

When the sky

grows dark at night,

I wish and wish

with all my might,

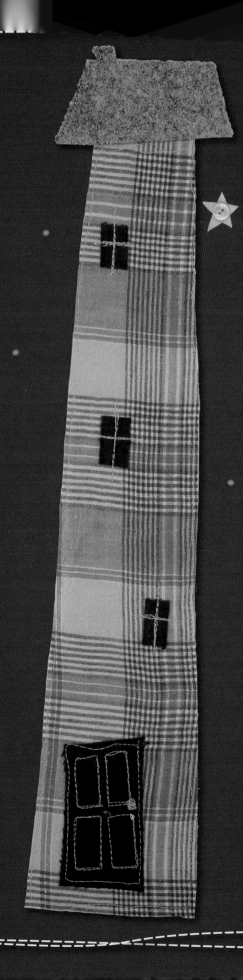

That you would look down
on my **house,**
And grant one thing
for this small **mouse.**

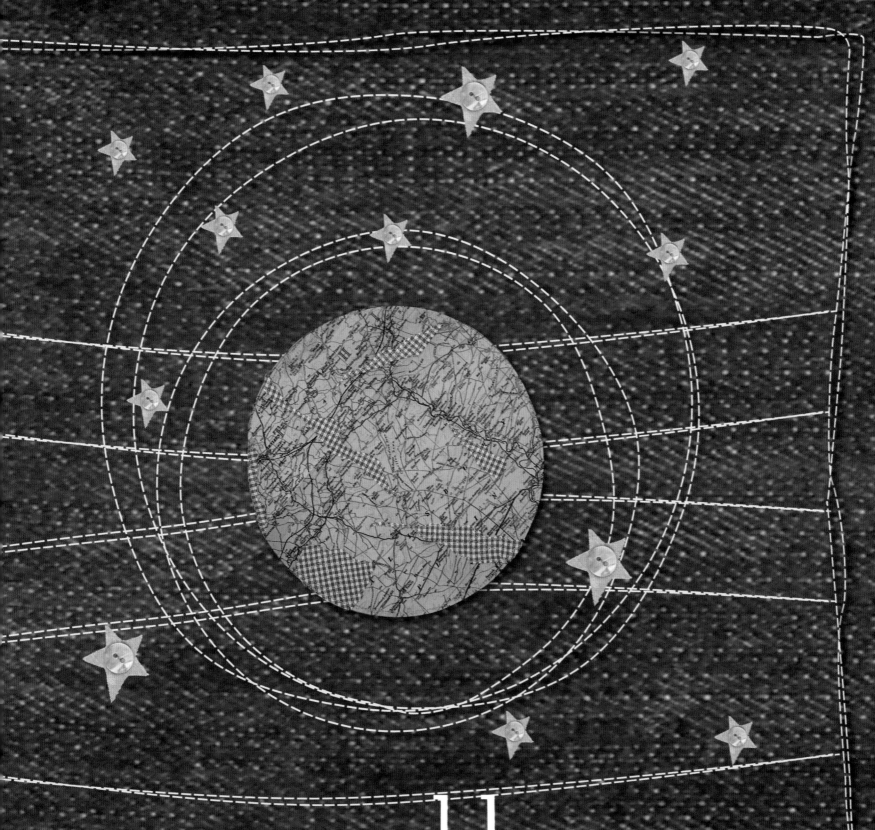

And see the world the way you do.

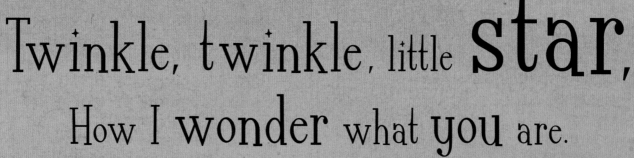

Twinkle, twinkle, little star,
How I wonder what you are.

stairs,

the

climb

time to

When it's

To brush my teeth
and say my prayers,

Through my window I can see,
That you are smiling down on me.

Twinkle, twinkle, little **star**, How I wonder what **you** are,